"WALLACE LOSES HIS BOOTS"

Text by James Drummond
Illustrations by Louise Annand

This book is dedicated to
Fiona, Andrew and Colvin

The author acknowledges the encouragement and advice given
by his friend, Station Officer James Smith of the Strathclyde Fire Brigade.
He also thanks the Staff of the Glasgow Room in the Mitchell Library
for their courtesy and help.

© James Drummond

Published in 1991 by
The Amaising Publishing House Ltd.
Musselburgh
EH21 7UJ
Scotland

031-665 8237

ISBN 1 871512 15 8

Printed & Bound by Scotprint Ltd, Musselburgh

Wallace was a polite dog. So when, one Saturday morning, Mr Jackson brought his children to visit College Street Fire Station, Wallace was the first to greet them, wagging his tail and looking up at them as if to say, "Good morning! I'm Wallace the Fire Dog. I'm in charge here and will be very pleased to show you round."

It was a very old building, and it felt quite dark and gloomy as they went through the archway, but a fire was burning brightly in the Watch Room. The fireman on duty, old Mr McGregor, gave them a friendly wave and a word of welcome.

And when Wallace led them into the sunny courtyard and proudly showed off one of his fire engines, bright scarlet and glittering with polished brasswork, they felt that the Fire Station was quite a cheerful place after all, even if it was very old.

The next place they visited was the Duty Room, where the firemen were waiting, ready to snatch up their helmets and pull on their big leather boots as soon as the alarm bell sounded.

The children were delighted to see the two pairs of small leather boots that Wallace sometimes wore when he went out with the fire engine. Mr McGregor had made them to protect his paws from the hard cobbled streets.

Snowy the cat looked as if she had boots as well, but of course these were just the chocolate coloured markings on her paws.

Wallace and Snowy got on quite well together — most of the time.

Just as the children got down to the shed where the fire engines were kept, they were startled by the loud clanging of a bell.

"It's the fire alarm," said their father. "We'd better stand back and keep out of everybody's way. This should be exciting."

It certainly was exciting — and very noisy too. Doors slammed all over the place. There was a sound like thunder from the stables as the horses drummed their hoofs on the door, impatient to be led out and harnessed to the fire engine. Then down from the Duty Room came the firemen, clumping and clattering on the narrow stairs.

The only quiet person was Wallace. He had barked once when the alarm bell went. Then, having wagged his tail vigorously to tell the visitors, "Sorry, but I've got to go now," he raced over to the fire engine and stood watching the men get ready to go off to the fire.

Each fireman knew exactly what he had to do, and they knew they had to do it quickly.

Two of the men led out the big horses, Kelvin and Clyde, and put them between the shafts. Another unbolted the street doors and pushed them back on their rollers. The fourth member of the team lit the fire under the boiler and used bellows to make the flames roar up fiercely. There had to be enough steam in the boiler to pump the water through the hoses as soon as they got to the fire.

Suddenly Wallace growled. Snowy the cat had wandered in to see what all the fuss was about. Wallace growled again. He seemed to be saying, "Go away Snowy! Or else . . ." Snowy went.

When the alarm bell rang there was no room in the Engine Shed for anybody except the firemen and their fire dog.

When the fire-fighting team had gone galloping off, with Wallace racing ahead barking loudly to warn everybody to get out of the way, Mr McGregor came to speak to the visitors.

"That was quick!" said Mr Jackson. He smiled. "I wish this lot could get off to school in the morning half as quickly."

"Oh, the men are quick all right", said Mr McGregor. "But we all wish we could do our turn-out just a wee bit faster. When there could be folk trapped in a burning building, every second counts. There's word that the Edinburgh fire brigade can turn out half a minute quicker than us. Maybe by the next time you visit us we'll be able to beat that record." And the Jacksons went away, well pleased with their exciting visit.

It had been quite a small fire, so it wasn't long before the men got back to the Fire Station. Wallace was pleased to see that some of the firemen's children were out playing in the courtyard. He hoped that he could join in the fun.

But first he had to help with the tidying up. The horses had to be rubbed down and led back into the stable. Three of the firemen unrolled the canvas hoses and hung them up to dry in the hose-tower, while others washed and polished the fire engine.

When all the work was finished, Mr Paterson, the captain of the fire-fighting team, went to report to his boss the Firemaster.

Firemaster Gilmour was hard at work in his office. In a few weeks time the firemen had to move to a bigger, more modern fire station, so the Firemaster was busy making a list of all the things that had to be done before the removal.

Wallace was busy playing with the children. First they played "Fetch it" — throwing a ball for Wallace to chase. But when they started a game of football, Wallace, being a sensible dog, knew to keep well clear of the bouncing ball and the kicking feet.

Snowy was not a sensible cat. Mr Paterson's son Jimmy was just about to score a very fine goal when Snowy somehow managed to get in between his left foot and his right foot. The ball went soaring into the air, crashed through the window and landed with a thump on the Firemaster's desk amidst a shower of shattered glass.

Wallace, looking very pleased with himself, burst into the office. He seemed to think that this was a new and exciting way of playing "Fetch it".

For once, Firemaster Gilmour was not pleased to see Wallace's happy face.

"You'd think we didn't have enough to do getting ready for this removal without you lot going around making more work," scolded the Firemaster. Jimmy's little sister Annie tried to explain that it was really Snowy's fault.

"Oh come on Annie!" exclaimed her Dad. "Don't tell me a wee cat kicked a big ball like that through the window!" The Firemaster joined in the laughter, but he still had some serious things to say.

"For the next few weeks the firemen are going to be far too busy to go around mending windows and cleaning up any mess you make. So you'd better find somewhere else to play. And do try to keep out of mischief."

Then Firemaster Gilmour put on his cap and strode round to Ingram Street, where the new Fire Station was being built. Wallace went with him.

Wallace had a great time sniffing around the new building. There were all kinds of strange and exciting smells — newly cut wood, hot melted tar, the workmen's morning pieces, sticky putty and fresh paint.

He found a fresh crust of bread. He snapped it up when the Firemaster wasn't looking and, as he got the nice taste of meat paste, he decided that he liked the new Ingram Street Fire Station.

The Firemaster was doing some hard thinking. "It's having to run down the stairs from the Duty Room that wastes the time," he muttered, half to himself, half to Wallace. "If only we could think of a quick way of getting down. . . ."

Wallace wagged his tail. "Don't worry," he seemed to say. "You'll think of something."

Next Saturday morning the children set off to play on Glasgow Green
— well away from busy firemen and troublesome cats. On the way they saw
some electric lamp-posts that had just been put up to replace the old gas ones.
It was Jimmy's idea to squeeze through the railings and slide down the lamp-
posts. It was a very silly idea, but it was good fun.

Then Annie thought up an even sillier idea. If you climbed up and stood
on the top of the railing you got a longer and faster slide to the pavement.
Unfortunately Annie's pinafore got caught on one of the spikes. She
couldn't get down and she couldn't get back. She was well and truly stuck.

Then it was Wallace's turn to have an idea. This time it was a good one.
He took to his heels and went racing back to the Fire Station to get help.

Mr Paterson was really angry. "Look what you've done!" he scolded. "You've made Mr McGregor call out an appliance that might be desperately needed for a fire. You've wasted the time of two very busy firemen. You've stopped the traffic on the High Street for half an hour . . ."

"And I've torn my pinny!" wailed Annie.

"Well, you can't blame Snowy this time," said Mr Paterson. "That cat's got more sense in its tail than you have amongst the lot of you!" And he went stamping back to the Fire Station to write his report.

When Firemaster Gilmour read the report in the log book his brows gathered in anger. But then he began to smile. He slapped his knee and reached for his cap.

"Come on Wallace!" he called. "We're off to Ingram Street again to see the builder. These children have just given me an idea."

At last the day came for the big removal. And what a busy day it was — especially for the horses. All day long the wagons and fire engines trundled along to the new Fire Station and then back again for another load. All the equipment had to be moved. Hoses and ladders, axes, ropes and fire escapes, brass helmets and heavy waterproof jackets, and all the other things that firemen need.

The children were busy too. Jimmy helped his father to load the furniture from their own home. Annie and her mum carefully packed the dishes in wooden boxes.

Wallace helped too, trotting alongside the horses, giving an occasional bark that seemed to say, "Cheer up! Trot on! Not many more loads now."

By late afternoon they were ready to make the last trip. Annie had to run back to say goodbye to the corner of the bedroom where she used to play with her dollies.

Then Wallace had to run back to sniff around till he found where Snowy was hiding. He chased her out to the waiting wagon.

Just as they were setting off, Mrs Paterson remembered a line of washing she had left in the drying room. So Jimmy had to run back to fetch that.

But at last they were ready to leave the old College Street Fire Station that had been their home for many happy years.

The most exciting thing about their new house was the bathroom. The bath had a copper boiler with a gas jet — rather like the brass boiler at the back of the fire engine. Mrs Paterson said that Jimmy and Annie would have a bath every Saturday night.

There was a neat little basin, so they wouldn't have to wash their hands in the kitchen sink, and a toilet with a comfy wooden seat and a china handle on the end of the chain. No more chilly trips down to the toilet in the courtyard!

Wallace was acting in a strange, anxious kind of way. Jimmy thought he might be worried in case he too had to have a bath every Saturday night.

The next day they discovered what was bothering Wallace. He was looking for his boots. Somehow or other they had gone missing during the removal.

Then Annie decided to give Snowy a nice bath in the new basin — and came back with the news that Snowy was missing too.

The third piece of bad news was that Jimmy couldn't remember where he had put the line of washing.

There was no time to search for all the missing things because Granny Paterson was coming to visit their new home. But, when Mr Paterson went to light the fire, Wallace startled everybody by standing in front of the fireplace, growling quite fiercely.

"Wallace *is* in a grumpy mood today," said Jimmy Paterson. "Don't worry old chap, we'll soon find your boots. Now — let's get the fire going."

But as soon as Mr Paterson struck the match Wallace leaped bodily into the fireplace, stuck his head and shoulders right up the chimney and scrabbled furiously with his forepaws.

"Oh my nice clean carpet!" moaned Mrs Paterson. "The dog's gone mad!" Annie was so frightened that she ran into the new bathroom and locked the door.

But Wallace was not mad. Down the chimney, into the fireplace and out onto the nice clean hearthrug tumbled a very dirty Snowy. Some cats get very upset and confused by removals. Snowy was one of them.

She made such a fuss about getting washed that Mr Paterson stuck her into one of his boots to stop her scratching.

Wallace was just about to get pushed into a soapy bath when the alarm bell rang. He scampered off, yelping happily as if to say, "Sorry! Can't stay for my bath. I've got fire-dog business to attend to."

A bad fire had broken out in the Western Club. This was a club for businessmen who worked in the city. Nobody could join unless they were wealthy and important. No women were ever allowed in — except of course the women who kept the place clean and tidy and cooked the big meals that the gentlemen ate.

It was Saturday afternoon. The gentlemen had finished a nice dinner of soup, fish, roast duck, mutton and steam pudding. Now most of them were snoozing in comfy armchairs until it was time to go home for their tea.

Unfortunately one of the snoozing gentlemen dropped his cigar into a waste paper basket. Very soon the curtains were blazing fiercely.

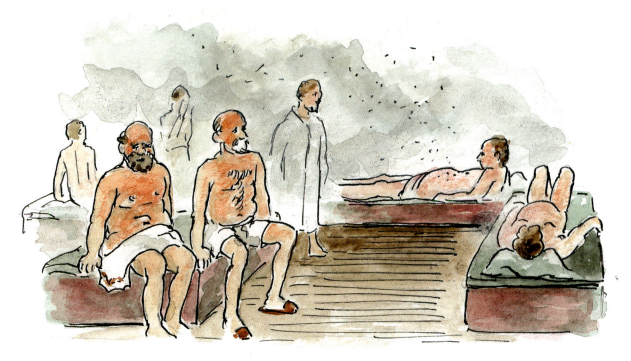

Some of the members spent their Saturday afternoons upstairs in the Turkish Bath. This was a special room filled with hot steam. The gentlemen would take off their smart city clothes and sit there getting hotter and damper and pinker every minute. They hoped that they were also getting thinner.

One of the gentlemen said, ''The steam's got a funny smell today.''

Another said, ''Why are there all these black smuts on my tummy?''

A third gentleman jumped up. ''Because it's not a steam bath we're having — it's a smoke bath! Fire! Help!''

Coughing and spluttering, sneezing and snorting, they made their way along the smoke filled corridor to the nearest window.

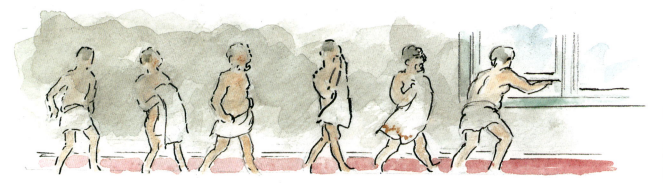

Fortunately the window was not very high, and some passers-by had very sensibly run into the club to get a carpet for them to jump into.

"Jump!" they shouted. "We'll catch you." The only trouble was that the gentlemen had no clothes on.

"Never mind that sir!" shouted a policeman. "Better catch a cold out here than get roasted like tatties in there. Jump into the carpet."

"Well, send all these people away!" demanded one of the trapped men. "Go away at once, all of you!"

But of course everybody wanted to see the important gentlemen jumping out of the window in their birthday suits. This was fine entertainment for a dull Saturday afternoon.

The trapped men were still jostling and arguing at the window when a chorus of excited shouts went up from the crowd.

"Here comes Wallace!" "Let the fire brigade through!" "Well done the fire dog!" "Hey Wallace! Have you no' got your boots today?"

Through a gap in the crowd scampered a rather grubby looking Wallace, closely followed by the fire engine. There was a loud cheer as the firemen ran out the extension ladder. Then a gasp of surprise, followed by an even louder cheer when out from the top of the ladder streamed a long rope with a lot of very colourful clothes pegged to it.

One of the trapped men reached out and grabbed hold of the biggest shirt. "I must say," he remarked, "our fire brigade thinks of everything!"

Of course it was the missing line of washing that Jimmy had hurriedly thrown into the wagon on the day of the removal. There was quite a scramble for the only pair of trousers on the line, and nobody really had much use for little Annie's winter vest, but it wasn't long before everybody had found something to fit them — more or less.

The spectators were delighted. This was even better than the circus on Glasgow Green, and it didn't cost them a penny.

But somebody didn't look at all happy about the fancy dress parade. Perhaps Wallace thought that people should not be laughing during a serious fire. Or perhaps he had been hoping that his lost boots would be found amongst the clothes.

A whole week went by and there was still no sign of Wallace's boots. They were lost. Mr McGregor looked out his cobbler's tools, but it takes time to make two pairs of boots for a dog, and before they were ready the day arrived for the Official Opening. About a hundred guests had been invited.

Glasgow's Lord Provost would be there, wearing his scarlet robes and gold chain. Edinburgh's Firemaster had sent a letter: "Thank you for the invitation. I am looking forward to seeing how quickly your men can turn out!" His wife had added a note saying how much she hoped to see Glasgow's famous fire dog wearing his famous boots.

Everybody in Ingram Street hoped they would find Wallace's boots in time. But as the day of the party arrived the hope faded.

Snowy wasn't making things any easier. All morning she had been behaving in a silly way and was managing to annoy everybody — especially Wallace. She ate half the dog's breakfast and dabbled her paw in his drinking water. When she jumped into his basket and started to scrabble the straw, Wallace decided that Snowy was really asking for trouble. And that he was going to give her some.

Snowy heard the "Watch it, cat!" growl and went streaking across the yard — straight into the coalshed. Wallace followed in a cloud of black coal dust.

There was a lot of clattering and rumbling, yowling, and snarling. Then the barking and growling suddenly changed to an excited yelp of surprise and delight.

Wallace had found his boots!

For once in his life Wallace made no protest about having a bath. They didn't even try to dust Snowy, because they knew that she would make too much of a fuss. And the first of the guests were beginning to arrive.

Wallace was ready just in time. Jimmy fastened on a brass collar made from the shoulder strap of his dad's old uniform, and Mr McGregor had given his boots a quick polish. He looked very smart.

The Firemaster of the Edinburgh Fire Brigade said that the Glasgow firemen looked very smart too. Then he added that they would have to move smartly as well if they hoped to beat a new turn-out record.

"My men can get away within eighty seconds of the alarm bell going," he boasted. "Do you really think that you can beat that?"

The Lord Provost looked a bit worried, but Firemaster Gilmour smiled quietly and said they would just have to try their best.

The Edinburgh Firemaster's wife was very elegant. After shaking hands with all the firemen she came over to speak to Mrs Paterson and the children.

Wallace had never seen such a big hat in his life before. He didn't particularly like her strong perfume, but her shoes had a nice leathery smell, so he sniffed them politely. She said some very nice things about his boots.

"What a nice little black cat," she remarked. "What is she called?"

"Please Miss, she's called Snowy," Annie answered. The lady looked puzzled.

"Snowy's a kind of nickname," explained Jimmy hastily. "Her real name is Sooty."

The Firemaster's wife said that she was sure the little black cat would bring them a lot of luck in the turn-out competition.

There was a buzz of excitement as the alarm bell rang for the start of the contest. Both Firemasters looked carefully at their watches.

Through in the Watch Room Mr McGregor pressed a blue button and the stable doors swung open, before the horses could even think of kicking them. Everybody clapped as Wallace trotted smartly out, closely followed by Kelvin and Clyde. Wallace sat down on a spot marked "W" and the horses obediently stopped too. Mr McGregor pressed a green button and the shafts of the fire engine dropped neatly over the horses' shoulders and fastened with a click.

Mr McGregor pressed a red button and hot gas flame set the water bubbling and the steam hissing in the brass boiler.

The fire engine was ready to move off. But where were all the firemen?

They seemed to come from nowhere, swiftly and silently sliding down the polished brass poles. It was brilliant! The audience clapped and cheered and little Annie was so excited that she called out, "Oh look! They're playing at our lamp-post game!" Everybody laughed, but she was right. That was exactly where the Firemaster had got his brilliant idea from.

Kelvin and Clyde's great hoofs struck showers of sparks on the cobbles as they followed Wallace out into Ingram Street.

The Edinburgh Firemaster was on his feet, waving his big gold watch in the air and shouting, "Magnificent! Just under forty seconds! That has to be a world record. Well done Glasgow!"

Then the Lord Provost got up on to a fire engine, straightened his gold chain, cleared his throat and began his speech.

It turned out to be rather a long speech and the children were quite relieved when his voice was suddenly drowned by the loud clatter of hoofs, the rumble of heavy wheels and the shrill blast of whistles. Wallace, Kelvin and Clyde and the firemen were back.

Unfortunately on the way they seemed to have collected about half the dogs in the neighbourhood. And now they came tumbling into the Fire Station, howling and yapping and rushing about in a high state of excitement.

The dogs were very friendly, but they made such a terrible noise that the Lord Provost quickly brought his speech to an end.

By the time Wallace had chased all the dogs away Mr Paterson was worrying in case the sausage rolls might be getting cold and the ice cream might be melting. So the Firemaster announced that the eating part of the Official Opening should begin and that there was no time for more speeches. Nobody seemed terribly disappointed.

As the guests enjoyed all the nice food that Mrs Paterson had prepared in her new kitchen, Wallace strolled about politely amongst them, picking up any old scraps of cheese or sausage meat or anything else that happened to fall — just to keep the new Fire Station nice and tidy, of course.

As a special treat the children were allowed to slide down the poles for ten minutes. As Firemaster Gilmour said, "After all, it was their idea in the first place!"

When everybody was going home after the party, the Edinburgh Firemaster's wife shook hands with all the children. Then she stroked Snowy and said, "Good-bye Sooty", and didn't notice that one of her white gloves had suddenly turned black.

She said it had been a lovely party. "Such a pity about those badly behaved dogs bursting in so impolitely. That sort of thing would never happen in Edinburgh, of course," she said. "But as for your dog Wallace — well, I think he must surely be the politest dog in Glasgow!"